STOP THE PRESSES!

Other Books By Dick Hyman

COCKEYED AMERICANA
TRENTON PICKLE ORDINANCE
LEST ILL LUCK BEFALL THEE
POTOMAC WIND AND WISDOM
IT'S THE LAW
BASEBALL WIT AND WISDOM
  (with Frank Graham)
FOOTBALL WIT AND HUMOR
  (with Gene Ward)
MARINE COMEDY
OF ALL FOOL THINGS
NONSENSE U.S.A.

STOP THE PRESSES!

THE BEST "SHORT TAKES" FROM THE PAGES OF "EDITOR & PUBLISHER,"

by

DICK HYMAN

ILLUSTRATED by **BOB DUNN**

INTRODUCTION by **ROBERT U. BROWN**

FOREWORD by **BOB CONSIDINE**

THE STEPHEN GREENE PRESS
Brattleboro, Vermont
Lexington, Massachusetts

FIRST PAPER EDITION 1982
Copyright © 1966 by Dick Hyman

This book is manufactured in the United States of America. It is published by The Stephen Greene Press, Fessenden Road, Brattleboro, Vermont 05301.

LIBRARY OF CONGRESS CATALOGING IN PUBLICATION DATA

Main entry under title:

Stop the Presses!

   Reprint. Originally published: New York: Hawthorne Books, 1966.

   1. American wit and humor.   I. Hyman, Dick, 1904-II. Editor & publisher.

[PN 6162.S89 1982]   081   82-5538
ISBN 0-8289-0475-8 (pbk.)   AACR2

CONTENTS

FOREWORD

If "To Err is Human," I've been working at a very human trade for half my life. Many changes have come through the years to the newspaper business: color, imaginative make-up, composition by means of bewildering black boxes, college-bred copy boys, and a proposal by one publisher (a Texan, naturally) to deliver his papers to outlying counties by Intermediate Range Ballistic Missile.

But one thing never changes: the typo.

Slips have been passing in the night since Johnny Gutenberg began playing lotto with his crazy movable types. There's no end to the boo-boos, most of them hilarious.

The most astonishing account of Pope Paul VI's historic one-day trip to New York on October 4, 1965, was my running news story as it appeared in the San Francisco *Examiner*. In the course of moving from the morning to the afternoon field in that delightful city, something happened to the ability of *Examiner* linotype machines to finish the last sentences of my paragraphs. Everything seemed to end with some word like "suddenly—".

Then there was the time I visited the home of Dr. Sam Sheppard, scene of the murder of his wife. I phoned in the story from a neighbor's home. The boy who took it at our INS bureau in Cleveland (and subsequently punched it and fed it into the main trunkline) turned out to be a spectacular speller.

I had dictated, in a description of the house, "The flotsam and jetsam of Lake Erie spill into the forlorn yard . . ."

It boomed out on the wire, "The flexum and gypsum of Lake Erie," etc.

The New Yorker magazine picked it up, "credited" me with it and concluded, "He may have been thinking of Sodom and Dannemora."

Great obscenities have appeared in remote classified ads—inserted by disgruntled printers—and have been clipped and carried in men's wallets with the care and attention usually afforded fragments of the Dead Sea Scrolls. I recall one such line in the Washington *Times-Herald* which so enraged the publisher, the incomparable Eleanor Patterson, that she called up her friend J. Edgar Hoover and asked him to put the FBI on the job.

The unconscious, the illiterate or the inadvertent gaff is much more to be treasured. There was the nice old maiden lady in the Society section of the Washington *Post* of yesteryear who wrote a memorable eight-column streamer to describe the busy social season the local belles were having during their Easter vacation. She wrote:

BALLS, BALLS, BALLS, BALLS IS ALL THE DEBUTANTES GET

A diplomat in an ink-stained paper hat coaxed her into changing it after the first edition. He explained to her that in the first run something had gone wrong with the hoe and it had broken every "L" in the place.

The same *Post* was once ordered by no less a figure than Woodrow Wilson to gather up and destroy every copy of its early edition. The President's indignation was understandable. He was courting the lovely widow Galt at the time, and the *Post's* story told in glowing terms how he had gallantly taken her on a sightseeing trip around Washington's governmental and historic showplaces during the day.

Alas, a vital syllable fell by the wayside, and startled readers read:

"The President spent the day entering Mrs. Galt."

I heard a harassed editor say recently, "Things in our shop are getting to a point where I'm afraid to send down a dozen corrections. You get back two dozen typos in the next edition."

This recalls the case of the irate retired colonel who stormed into a paper in a great fume one day. It seems that a compliment-laden feature referred to him as "battle-scared" instead of "battle-scarred." An urgent correction was rushed through. The replate called him "bottle-scarred."

The year a fine blond boy named Don McNeill won the National Singles tennis championship I started my lead, "Tow-headed Don McNeill today won etc. etc." It came out "Two-headed" in the *Mirror*.

But who am I to complain? I got into this glorious business partly through a typo. I was working in the Government as a typist at the time, and had reached the third round of an obscure tennis tournament in Washington. The agate "other results" shirttail on the *Herald*'s story had me down as "Bob Constantine." Fresh punk that I was, I went down to the *Herald* to set the record straight. I don't recall ever leaving it. I had found Valhalla (and let's see what the composing room does with good old Val).

BOB CONSIDINE

INTRODUCTION

Prof. Henry Higgins' lament to Eliza Doolittle was: "Why can't the English teach their children how to speak?"

A parallel utterance from many modern parents is: "Why can't my children learn to spell?"

Since the spelling of many English words bears absolutely no resemblance to phonetics, it is no wonder that the language is frequently murdered in print.

Combine mental lapses with the vagaries of a mechanical monster which is designed to transform the finger-tip touch on a keyboard into alphabetical characters on a lead slug ready for printing and you have what is commonly called "a typographical error." The number of words that have two or more meanings compound the possibilities for error.

No one has yet determined a formula to establish what percentage human error and what part mechanical failure are required to produce a typographical error. It has been determined, however, that the English language is made to order for this phenomenon because of the vast number of words whose meanings can be altered, for better or worse, by the addition, omission or transposition of a character.

Editor & Publisher, the newsmagazine of the newspaper business, has published weekly for more than thirty-five years a selection of the most humorous boners of this kind that have appeared across the nation.

It is from this grist of thousands of items that Dick Hyman has culled the best for this book.

ROBERT U. BROWN
Editor & Publisher magazine

9

NEWS BREAKS

Oftentimes, in the rush of things on the presses of your local newspaper, someone commits a typographical error. Here are some we have picked up from the pages of *Editor & Publisher.*

Movie guide in the Boston (Mass.) Traveler describes: the new Alec Guinness comedy in which he plays a sailor with a girl in two parts.

Associated Press filler as received by the Rochester (N.Y.) Democrat & Chronicle: A bashful beau scratched "I love you honey" on the trunk lid of the girl.

From Drew Pearson's column in the Corpus Christi (Tex.) Caller: He began life driving a mule in a coal mine.

Bathers sought refuge away from the fire on the wet side of the lake—*Syracuse (N.Y.) Herald American.*

Sun bathing is hard to explain. You either see it or you don't—*Boston (Mass.) Post.*

He was rushed to a hospital where he was pronounced dead on arrival but gave officers a description of his assailant—*San Jose (Calif.) News.*

No governor in many years has been able to love on the salary paid him—*Wildwood-by-the-Sea (N.J.) Leader.*

One of the most interesting events for ladies will take place when there will be a petting and approach contest on the golf course—*Wildwood-by-the-Sea (N.J.) Star and Wave.*

An International bathing contest will continue under another name—without bathing suits—*New York Herald Tribune.*

The dark-haired legal dynamo's hazel eyes sparkled as she declared: "I became interested in divorce the day I met my husband"—*Miami (Fla.) Daily News.*

Birth announcement in the South Bend (Ind.) Tribune: Mr. and Mrs. D—— H——, Barrien Springs, eight pound, eight ounce son, Dec. 20 at 5:45 a.m. tried the new method this past season expressed satisfaction with it and indicated plans to try more of it next year."

The night trunk wire of the United Press carried this dispatch from Eufaula, Alabama: A mother who already has six children, today gave birth to a four-room, unpainted house set back in a tenant farmer's cotton field.

We had been married only a few weeks when I discovered to my joy that Norman had the makings of a real husband—*Springfield (Ohio) Daily News.*

The new Miss America will be drowned later before a nationwide television audience—*AP report from Atlantic City (N.J.)*

A woman offered $10 to kiss George Jessel at a fundraising rally. George then killed 152 women and raised $1,520—*Raleigh (N.C.) News & Observer.*

The woman's body was found after two fishermen discovered her in their shack, cooking breakfast, and told police—*Columbus (Ga.) Enquirer.*

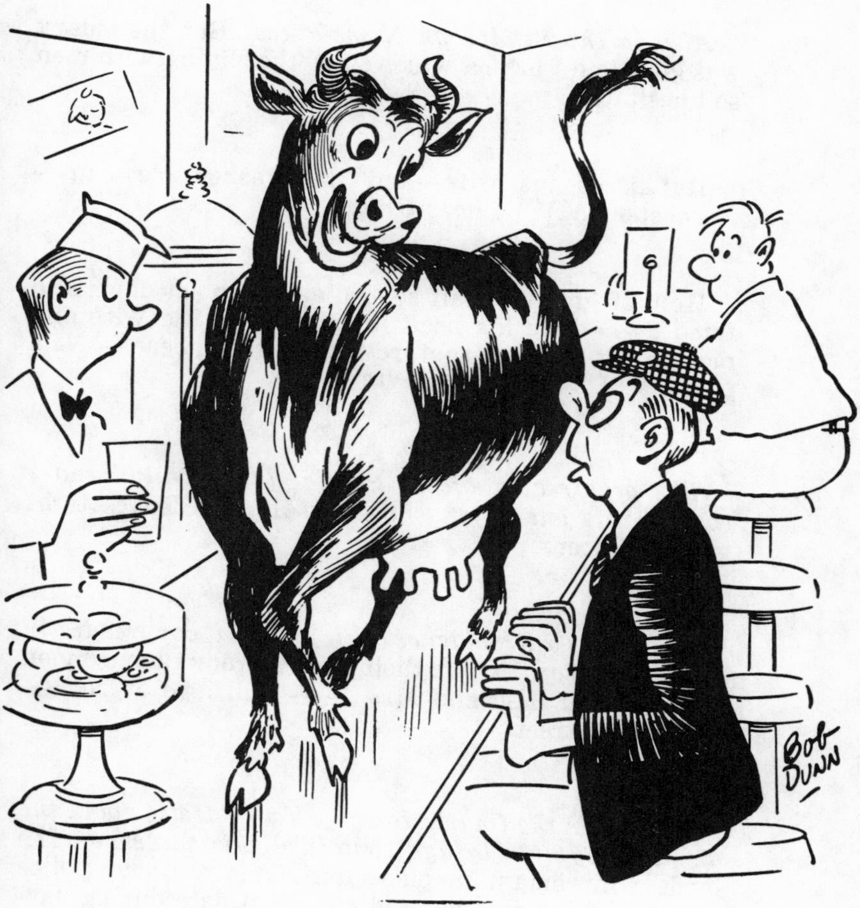
BOB DUNN

North Carolina Department of Agriculture handout, as released and carried over the AP wire: Milk now sold in public eating places must be in original containers.

The service opened with the vocal hymns "Lead Kindly Light" and "I Need Three Every Hour"—*St. Joseph (Mo.) News-Press.*

Also in the St. Joseph News-Press: But the salary was good and I have a widowed mother living with men so I hesitated.

He kissed his wife—and the washer blew up—*Rochester (N.Y.) Times-Union.*

He half groaned, half sobbed and then sat down and fried as he held his head in his hands. His wife and mother sat in the front row with their heads—*New Orleans (La.) States and Item.*

The proofreader of the Pontiac (Ill.) Daily Leader caught this one in an obituary: He also leaves tight grandchildren.

Caught by a Providence (R.I.) Journal copyreader in a wedding story: Upon their return from a honeymoon in the South, Mr. and Mrs. —— will love at No. —— Ferncrest Street.

A story in the Charleston (W. Va.) Gazette about the dismantling of a bridge contained this sentence: The bride will remain in place until July 2 under police protection and may be used until that date during daylight hours for visits to the park.

Obituary in the Streator (Ill.) Times-Press: Burial will be made in a cemetery where she formerly lived.

Lead to travel story in the St. Petersburg (Fla.) Evening Independent: If you want to go to Bermuda by air, take a plane. That's the best way to travel through the air.

Suicide story in the Contra Costa (Calif.) Gazette related how a man leaped from an 11th-floor window: after fighting off the efforts of a pretty elevator operator to have him.

Inductee story in the Pontiac (Ill.) Daily Leader: The platform was crowded with sweethearts and parents. Only one of the group was married.

Accident story in the New Brunswick (N.J.) News: The bus crunched through the front door of a tavern, injuring four men heated at the bar.

Personal mention in the Gallup (N. Mex.) Independent: Mrs. Blank returned Thursday night from San Francisco. Her husband returned the same night from Pine River dam where he wished without luck for four days.

Caught in proof by the Mission (Tex.) Times: John Blank passed away last week. Our best wishes to him for a speedy recovery.

Story in the Kitchener-Waterloo (Ont.) Record quoting the director of the Miss Canada pageant, stating that girls will be judged in evening dresses rather than bathing suits: "I have fought for five years to get the bathing suits off the girls," he said.

Associated Press report received by the Schenectady (N.Y.) Union Star: President Truman said that his executive oder tightening control over government information grew out of the publication of secrets, etc.

Personality sketch in the Houtzdale (Pa.) Citizen Standard: He has been afflicted with the Republican party for the last 18 years.

Geography described by the Milwaukee (Wis.) Sentinel: Patricia was born in St. Louis while her parents were living in Woodriver, Illinois.

Personal item in the Hudson (N.Y.) Daily Star: Mr. Smith, who has been very ill for the past week, is still under the car of Dr. Jones.

From a Kansas newspaper: A woman was overcome by gas while taking a bath but owes her life to the watchfulness of her janitor.

Fire drill described by the Hopewell (Va.) News: A ladder demonstration was also given in which firemen carried a horse to the top of the ladder.

Police story in the Solano (Calif.) Republican: Police Chief Clift, who was wearing hightop boots and was minus his uniform, exhibited his credentials.

News story in the Greensboro (N.C.) Daily News: A Census Bureau report revealed today that Southern girls do marry at an early urge.

Description of a new house by the Lubbock (Tex.) Avalanche Journal: The panty has a vent at the floor and one in the ceiling. During warm weather the floor vent can be opened. Cool air rushes in and forces the warm air out.

Announcement in the Oxford (Ohio) Press: Mr. and Mrs. Joe Doakes are the parents of a baby girl, following an accident in the apartment.

Concert review in the Winfield (Kan.) Courier: As an encore, Miss Brown played the old favorite "Carry Me Back to Old Virginity."

Description in the Pittsburgh (Pa.) Press of the inauguration of Gov. John S. Fine outdoors in a freezing rain: Mr. Fine wore a bow tie—all he ever wears.

The Spokane (Wash.) Spokesman-Review reports that a man was: wounded in the elbow and treated in the suburb.

Marysville (Calif.) Appeal-Democrat: They think that nothing matters except that they thrill to each other's ouch, and they never doubt but that they will go on billing and cooing forever.

Schnozzle wreck reported in the Bellefontaine (Ohio) Examiner: He escaped from his demolished automobile with only a scratch on his nose after it had left the road, and struck a fence, a tree, a sign, a concrete culvert and a rock along U.S. Route 68.

Associated Press report from Davenport (Iowa): Mervin A. Fulton, who has been associated with the Dallas Times for 41 years, has taken over the cuties of editor of the Times.

Caught by a proofreader of the Grand Forks (N. Dak) Herald: Mother's joy is in giving not conceiving.

Shaving advice in the Coatesville (Pa.) Record: Most men make the mistake of not washing their faces thoroughly with hot soup and water before they begin shaving.

Home hint in the Western Family magazine: When she washes dishes, he should wash dishes with her, and when she mops up the floor, he should mop up the floor with her.

Hot-weather quote in the Evansville (Ind.) Courier: She's no good; she had a record as long as my arm, reaching from California to North Carolina.

When, as is his custom, Senator Goldwater referred to Defense Secretary Robert S. McNamara as "Yo-yo," a man in the crowd yelled: "Give 'em hell, Barry." This loyal ally was ousted and then murdered—*New York Herald Tribune.*

In the Syracuse (N.Y.) Herald-Journal: In fact he had booked passage on a flight home for himself and souse.

L.B.J.'s charming daughter, Luci Baines, will be seen on the TV show in two parts—*Chicago Daily Tribune.*

He died of a cerebral grocery store on Connecticut hemorrhage—*Washington (D.C.) Evening Star.*

20

Story about a minister in the Muncie (Ind.) Morning Star: He also did graduate work at the Union Cemetery, New York.

Eulogy offered up by the Pomeroy (Ohio) Democrat: For 59 years he practiced medicine, being responsible for most of the babies born in this community.

Barbershop news in the Columbus (Ohio) Citizen: When Miss Smith awakened to find a burglar at her bedside, she gave him a shave and screamed for help.

At Boca Raton, where he will go by motorcycle, President Johnson will speak at dedication of Florida Atlantic University—*Associated Press.*

Knowland spoke first to an audience for Goldwater who overflowed the banquet room for a fun-raising dinner—*Richmond (Va.) Times-Dispatch.*

Men's fashions, as reported in the Knoxville (Tenn.) Sentinel: Ten years ago a gentleman wouldn't consider anything but pure white cotton shorts. . . . Now the same man not only welcomes color but actually enjoys frivolity in his drawers.

From the Radio-Television Daily: Eva Gabor is not about to stick that pipe in her mouth—or any place else for that matter.

Oklahoma City (Okla.) Times: The bride is bolted together in sections and moved forward on rollers.

Walter Winchell quoted the New York Mirror as stating: Former Secretary of State Dean Acheson arrived for a sex vacation.

Quote from the Ithaca (N.Y.) Journal: He felt the Canadian beauty at her apartment and went home.

Story in the Reading (Pa.) Times: Stalin is said to have remarked once that he was more oriental than accidental.

The woman's body was discovered by a janitor under the bed—*Medford (Oreg.) Mail Tribune.*

22

Stunned, dead passengers crawled from the wreckage—*Los Angeles Daily News.*

Item in the Reno (Nev.) State Journal: The Humane Society in 1952 housed 2,195 dogs, 3,200 cats, two monkeys and a politician, two monkies and a pelican.

Item in the Minneapolis (Minn.) Sunday Tribune: Miss Blank, young high school teacher, tendered her resignation rather than be reloved by the school board.

Drive carefully—the wife you save may be your own —*Thompsonville (Conn.) Press.*

Story about a 19-year-old bridge in the Wabash (Ind.) Plain Dealer: The bride is in good condition. It should be, residents point out, because it has hardly ever been used.

Paul Ellis' United Press story came out this way in the Columbus (Ohio) Citizen: A study by three physicians showed today that perhaps two out of three births in the United States result from pregnancies.

Describing an Indian encampment, a Wichita (Kans.) Eagle reporter wrote: An Indian woman squatted over a fire in one tepee, and you could smell fresh meat cooking.

Social item from the Vancouver (B.C.) News Herald: Masks must be worn, but dress is optional.

Understatement of her situation by Mrs. Lewis Miller, Tazewell, Va., whom AP reported as saying: "I shot him because he had me down and was beating me. I hope he won't die but if he does I will never live with him again."

Letters to Santa Claus as published in the Wellington (Tex.) Leader weekly included: Dear Santa, I am a little boy six years old. . . . I would like a steam shovel and a truck with a wench like Daddy's.

Caption on an AP wirephoto out of Cleveland:
Blizzard Baby—Teri Ann, Cleveland's "blizzard baby," shown above with her mother, Mrs. Harry Zellman, will be two years old Sunday. The child was born in the snow in a hospital parking lot unnoticed by her father and mother, who collapsed as she stepped from an automobile.

Excerpt from a New York Post crime story: Ray fired one shot. The two cops stepped out from behind the pillar and let go. Farrager fell dead, riddled with bullets. Farrager dashed by the patrolmen and made his getaway.

The Waco (Tex.) Messenger, in reporting social news from nearby Odessa, stated: St. John Baptist Church, Rev. L.M. Brown, Pastor: The members met with the pastor in bed in the pastor's home and had a lovely meeting; reports were good; amount $37.80.

On the bulletin board in the National Press Club was this notice for a chorus rehearsal: All club members who can sin are invited to join up.

Faces of a reporter and the city editor of the Jersey City (N.J.) Journal flushed when readers demanded an apology for this: T——, who was born in Jersey City and came to the United States in 1904 . . .

This unusual twist to a fatal shooting appeared in the Princeton (Ky.) Leader: She said the dead man appeared at her front door and demanded admittance.

Hold your seat! An item in the Huntington (N.Y.) Long-Islander about a new Long Island Railroad time-table reported: Most trains leave for the East and West the same time.

The room was examined and photographed and the brassiere was searched for clues—*Philadelphia (Pa.) Inquirer.*

The following notice appeared in the Arab (Ala.) News: On next Wednesday evening, the Ladies Aid will hold a rummage sale at the Methodist Church. Good chance to get rid of anything not worth keeping, but too good to be thrown away. Bring along your husbands.

The United Press carried this dispatch: Chardon, Ohio—The Geauga Republican Record carried a correction in this week's issue. It follows: "There was a mistake in an item sent in two weeks ago which stated that Adrian Welsh entertained a party at crap shooting. It should have been trap shooting."

A *woman lecturer on dress reform was shocked at the report of one of her speeches that appeared in the Lakewood (Ohio) Times. The story concluded with:* The lady lecturer on dress wore nothing that was remarkable. *But somewhere along the type route a period was inserted, so that the published story was concluded:* The lady lecturer on dress wore nothing. That was remarkable.

From the Zanesville (Ohio) Signal: The Lancaster Band Director has prepared an appalling program.

Martinsburg (W. Va.) Journal: With 23½ pints, the two ladies were high players in four tables of duplicate bridge.

Tallahassee (Fla.) Capital Post: Internal Revenue officials said they may be able to help confuse taxpayers struggling with their income tax forms.

Mrs. Joe B——, who is ill in Glendale Hospital, has not been so well—*Moundsville (W. Va.) Daily Echo.*

She was given a sedative and told to rest by a doctor—*Oakland (Calif.) Tribune.*

He is not very old because he started when he was a mere boy—*Louella Parsons' column in the New York Journal-American.*

She made an unscheduled and sudden departure from the saddle, head first, into the drink. Her mouth stayed behind—*Atlanta (Ga.) Journal.*

Her mouth twisted downward and suddenly her composure was gone and she was sobbing and screaming in muted agony—*New York Journal-American.*

He reads without glasses and only gave up spitting firewood last year—*Chicago Tribune.*

He was found unconscious by a neighbor who smelled gas and two maintenance men—*St. Petersburg (Fla.) Times.*

29

An empty bottle containing sleeping pills was found
—*Philadelphia (Pa.) Inquirer.*

Weather, as reported by the Roanoke (Va.) World-News: Partly cloudy and mild today 35. Sunday, cloudy followed by night.

Richmond (Va.) News-Leader: The three men make and repair the 5,000 Venetian blonds used throughout Richmond's 56 public schools.

Chicago (Ill.) Sun-Times: Metropolitan Opera officials ordered alterations on a performance gown they found too darling around the bosom.

Judge described in the Minneapolis (Minn.) Star: Judge Blank, silver-haired and suntanned, keeps himself in physical condition by daily setting-up exercises and twice-weekly trips to the YWCA.

Portland (Oreg.) Oregonian: Tomorrow we may expect strong northwest winds reaching a gal in exposed places.

Lead to beauty contest story in the Seneca (S.C.) Journal: Little gals, medium sized gals and big gals, all of Oconee's most beautiful bellies, will be the bill of fare Thursday night.

New Bedford (Mass.) Standard-Times: Our Mayor needs your cooperation. This is an emergency. Use the bus. Save your clutch and rear end.

Long Island (N.Y.) Star-Journal: It's just disgusting to see women wear lipstick above their hip line.

Jackson (Miss.) State-Times: Sunday breakfast meeting has been planned for the official board of the church, with the Rev. Mr. Blank undressing the group.

From a report of the American Psychological Association's convention in the San Francisco Examiner: Women who are cooperative and good sports are more likely to have large families.

Portland (Ind.) Graphic: A check at the local swimming pool revealed some startling figures.

From a garden club magazine: She is an expert gardener. Her chrysanthemums in the autumn are a subtle joy; her lips in the spring are thrilling.

Los Angeles Mirror-News: What's he like? Well, he has a worm personality and a low, pleasant voice.

Personal in the Wabash (Ind.) Plain Dealer: Mrs. Blank underwent surgery Wednesday in the Woodlawn Cemetery.

Crawfordsville (Ind.) Journal and Review: Members are urged to bring any eligible women who might wish to become mothers.

Sales News in the Anamosa (Iowa) Journal: Cattle, hogs, children, machinery, and equipment will be sold.

Muncie (Ind.) Evening Press: Desires to avoid having children at her wedding.

Wedding bells in the Houston (Tex.) Press: She got worried over the week-end and left on a honeymoon.

Sault Ste. Marie (Mich.) Evening News: He once fed horses up to $1\frac{3}{4}$ pounds a day and they still chewed on fence posts and managers.

Tulsa (Okla.) Tribune: The safety pin was removed after his parents took him to the divan when he swallowed the hospital.

A rural correspondent sent this paragraph to the Gloversville (N.Y.) Morning Herald: Mrs. John B——— presented her husband with an eight-pound baby girl on Thursday. Mrs. B——— was formerly Miss Anna

G—— and very popular locally. The happy parents have the congratulations of all on this suspicious event.

All local records for stopping the press were made in 1938 in William Allen White's Emporia (Kans.) Gazette office when it was discovered that the make-up man had mixed up the standing heads and put the one belonging to the road report, Highways and Detours, *over the* Deaths and Funerals *column.*

The following appeared in the Hazelton Independent, a weekly, shortly after North Dakota had joined the ranks of the wet states:

NO LIQUOR FOR EDITORS

The coming of hard, red "likker" means nothing to the editors of North Dakota's newspapers, for it is written that they can't afford to buy it in the first place, and in the second place it has been found to have a very decided effect upon the clearness of their grey matter—commonly known as brains—for one editor tried it with dire results. Someone sent one of our illustrious and brilliant editors a bottle of liquor. The same day he received for publication a wedding announcement and a notice of an auction sale. The "red likker" and the typewriter failed to function in harmony, with the following results:

"William Smith and Miss Lucy Andersen are to be disposed of at a public auction at my farm one mile east of a beautiful cluster of roses on her breast and two white calves, before a background of farm implements too numerous to mention in the presence of about seventy guests, including two milch cows, six mules and one bobsled. Rev. Jackson tied the nuptial knot with two hundred feet of hay wire on the bridal left on one good John Deere gang plow for an extended trip with terms to the purchaser. They will be at home to their friends with one good baby buggy and a few kitchen utensils after date of sale to responsible parties and some fifty chickens."

IN THE PUBLIC NOTICE

The classified advertising section of almost any newspaper often proves that some people either have a contorted sense of humor or are careless with their choice of words.

Cherry Valley (N.Y.) News: Man to shovel snow with twin beds.

Dallas (Tex.) Times-Herald: Twin-sized mattresses urgently needed.

Jersey City (N.J.) Journal: Woman wanted as housekeeper; no clothing.

Belen (N. Mex.) News: Wanted—Salesgirl. Must be respectable until after Christmas.

Miami (Fla.) Herald: Double twin beds, with privileges.

Green Bay (Wis.) Press Gazette: Attractive Sleepin Groom.

Schenectady (N.Y.) Union Star: Widow desires girl to share home or gentleman.

Advertising copy in the Tucson (Ariz.) Daily Star:
Don't kill your wife! Let our Bendix washing machine
do your dirty work.

In the Trenton (N.J.) Evening Times: Woman—
wants cleaning every Friday.

For rent—three room apartment. No drinking children or pets—*Champaign-Urbana (Ill.) Courier.*

3 Men to help install electric unit, and one office
girl—*Hilo (Hawaii) Tribune-Herald.*

Room with broad for one or two—*Newark (N.J.)
Evening News.*

Everything furnished, $10 for two girls—*Wichita
(Kans.) Eagle & Beacon.*

For sale—occasional chair by lady with carved,
clawed feet—*Cactus (Ariz.) Sage.*

Wanted—man to burn in scrap yard—*Lancaster
(Pa.) Sun News.*

*A stenographic need by Topeka, Kansas, newspapers
was reported in an ad in the Topeka State Journal
thus:* . . . have an immediate opening for a first class
stenographer, preferably one with some business sex-
perience.

Idaho (Boise) Evening Statesman: Wanted 2 mature
ladies for solicitation.

The following advertisement appeared in the Elberton (Ga.) Star: Notice. This is to certify that I know the forked-tongued, snake-eyed skunk that killed my Doberman Pinscher dog in cold blood. I certainly know

the "Judy Hole" in the Savannah River where he took a rock and tied it to him and sank him in twenty feet of water to keep the buzzards away so that I could not find him. If the man will have the nerve to come to me and admit it, I will give him $10 provided he will be able to put it in his pocket when I get through with him. And I don't mean maybe.

*One in the Watertown (N.Y.) Times says a tailor is
selling suits at a special price:* With extra pants to
match. Better hurry. They won't last long.

*Another ad in the Syracuse (N.Y.) Herald-Journal
has a jeweler advertising the:* Best Bum in town. The
watch with plus value.

Livestock wanted by an advertiser in the Plant City (Fla.) Courier: Want to buy small horse. Must be gentle and able to work. Also do auto repairing.

Classified ad in the Atlanta (Ga.) Constitution under "Rooms with Board": Vacancy for gentleman, both single and double. Also lady to share room. References exchanged.

Classified under "Antique and Restoration" in St. Petersburg (Fla.) Times: Figures and busts reduced. Sensational reduction of other things. Imported old bags at your own prices.

A cook—Live in. Private room and bath. Meals, laundry, good natured people to live with. Will lend

Clinton (Iowa) Herald: For sale: One Hollywood twin bed. Also want to buy one dog house in good condition.

New Albany (Miss.) Gazette: Lost: One end of baby on Highway 15.

Denver (Colo.) Rocky Mountain News: Wanted— Counter girl for dry cleaning children.

Dallas (Tex.) Times-Herald: Young engineer desires apartment. Bachelor. No children.

In the Brantford (Ont.) Expositor: Man with necessary equipment to spread manure.

From the Talbotton (Ga.) New Era: Sheer stockings. Designed for dressy wear, but so serviceable that lots of women wear nothing else.

Read in the Stockton (Calif.) Record: Home privileges, good food, women.

Front apartment, shower bath and one lady—*Lexington (Ky.) Herald.*

Two bedroom home. Blonds and drapes go with the price—*Sarasota (Fla.) Journal.*

Classified from the Fort Worth (Tex.) Press: If the lady whose girdle I wore away by mistake call 6-3354 I will gladly exchange.

diamonds, mink coat for one day off each week. Will exchange references—*a Wanted-Female column in the Kingston (N.Y.) Freeman.*

A classified ad appearing on page one in the Lamar (Mo.) Democrat recently read: Wanted: Someone to stay with my wife, mostly at night. Good wages.

Ad in the Watervliet (Mich.) Record in 1946: For sale—Outdoor toilet made of good lumber when Democrats were Democrats and Republicans were Republicans; not New Deal splinters.

The publisher of the Seminole (Okla.) Producer ran an ad in the Daily Oklahoman for: Reporter, male or female, MUST BE ABLE TO READ AND WRITE.

In a well-known New York City newspaper, a classified ad appeared for: Chambermaids . . . full of part time.

Big shepherd dog; must have large bushy tail that wags constantly for sweeping purposes at Mayfair Hotel. Maids have gone to war—*in Grand Island (Nebr.) Independent.*

These ads in the classified columns of the Grand Junction (Colo.) Sentinel:
Not responsible from this date for any debts contracted by my wife—(Signed) J.A.S.
He never did, why now?—(Signed) E.L.S.

In the Detroit (Mich.) Free Press: I am not responsible for anything my wife gets.

Decatur (Ill.) Review: Wanted. Used secretary in good condition.

Spring came to Florida and this want ad to the Miami (Fla.) Herald: Lost—Sat. night between 320 and 545 NW 29th Street, blue Japanese silk pajama bottom.

The Publishers' Auxiliary on January 2, 1943 carried this classified gem under "Help Wanted, Editorial": Girl journalism graduate with at least a year's weekly experience on news and ads needed badly to assist publisher of good weekly. Prefer girl who is perfect 36, beautiful, smart, willing to work for $5 a week, interested in weekly papers, Protestant, Catholic, Jewish, white or colored. Because of war we might waive some or all preferences. Office is cold in winter, hot as hell in summer, the toughest weekly joint in the state to work in because we're ornery. We also expect perfection in other folks. We serve beer when the 40-year-old press has a birthday and serve sarcastic remarks anytime. You'll suffer here, but you'll be a newspaper man or fired before you go, so don't come for a two-month holiday. We just finished making a swell newspaper man out of a guy with a Wisconsin M.A., but right now he wants to sleep in Navy hammocks. Of course, if can cook, too, or use a speed graphic it wouldn't hurt, but you don't have to sweep the floors or wash windows or melt metal. If you want to take a chance, tell us something about yourself and what you read and what your plans are. If you've got questions, ask 'em. We don't want you here only two weeks any more than you want to get fired or quit. We've got the swellest staff in the state, or did have until the war, and we want to keep half-way good. (Oh yes, don't worry. My wife can cook good.) Geo. W. Greene, Leader News, Waupum, Wis.

●

An ad in the Las Vegas (Nev.) Evening Review Journal for the Victory Sandwich Shop frankly stated: We cater exclusively to drunks and winos. We specialize in sobering foods of the finest quality, guaranteed not to warp, shrink or buckle. Our prices are subject to change while eating. We have no competition—never lost a drunk.

And in the Minneapolis (Minn.) Star Journal was this ad under personal: To Pete's girl friend—will turn him over to you soon. Hope you have better luck with him than I did. His wife.

In a story based on the ad, the Star Journal told the wife's side of the matter and advised: Watch for the girl friend's answer.

A moving and storage company in Chicago placed the following classified ad in a Chicago newspaper: Our help are all tired—so unless you need anything real bad, do not come this week.

Help wanted—Girls and women wanted on life preservers to bring our boys back—*Worcester (Mass.) Telegram.*

Married dairy hand to strip behind milking machine—*San Antonio (Tex.) Express.*

An unnamed citizen inserted this classified ad in the Palestine (Tex.) Herald: Your dog ain't getting much out of my garbage pail, so why don't you feed him.

Apartment hunting in Fresno, California, is really whacky, as witness this ad from the Fresno Bee: Half-wit vet, 3 dogs, 4 cats, a chronic alcoholic, wife and small monster on the way, desires a small apt. to practice his homework. Major at FSC house wrecking, intends to take up drums.

Apartment wanted immediately by man expecting first baby—*an ad in the Montreal (Que.) Star.*

Lady clerk for store, with kitchen and bedroom privileges if necessary—*Brantford (Ont.) Expositor.*

Mattress in use only a few weeks and large diamond engagement ring—*Merced (Calif.) Sun Star.*

Large bedroom between two trolleys. Near town—*Shreveport (La.) Journal.*

It pays to advertise, Claude Kastner, of Nebraska City, Nebr., agrees. Someone stole his overcoat and he inserted this ad in the Nebraska City News-Press: I wish a Merry Christmas to the person who stole my coat.

The next day he got his coat in the mail.

This one is on Editor & Publisher—excerpt from a Salesman Wanted ad in the November 3, 1945, issue: Salary $125,000 per week and possibly more if the candidate has extra special qualifications.

A classified ad in the Ogden (Utah) Standard-Examiner was as follows: Owner of 1940 Ford [this was in 1942] would like to correspond with widow who owns two tires. Object, matrimony. Send pictures of tires.

Short Takes got its answer when it repeated the Ogden Standard-Examiner ad. The answer to the Ogden paper from Salem, Oregon, reads: Gentlemen: This ad was handed to me (a widow) for three years, by death. And that the 13th a good date to try my luck. If this "guy" is no longer interested (don't know how old the ad is) perhaps you know of someone who is. I have more than two tires—will have picture taken when I know to where it is to be sent. Hope someone opens this letter who is as ready for "fun" as I am. Yours truly, Mrs. P. H., 17 Gerth Avenue, Salem, Oregon. P.S. My age, 62, weight, 145, 5 feet 5 inches. Tires are young yet—and don't known why.

Signs of the times—a classified ad in the Austin (Tex.) Tribune: Notice to car thieves: My tires are puncture-proof. If you try to steal them, you had better be puncture-proof too.

The following ad was published in the Portsmouth (Ohio) Times: Theft reported. Party who stole my suit out of store may have extra trousers. Call and get them at store. No questions asked. E. S. Farver, manager, 630 Second.

The Princeton (W. Va.) Observer received the following classified advertisement from H. H. Skaggs, clerk in the Princeton Post Office: I will pay $5 reward to any party who will admit to my wife that he threw the whiskey bottles in my garden.

From the Pike County (Pa.) Times: School teacher with concealed radiators wishes to rent room for winter months. Allergic to feather mattresses, flowers and fly spray.

Classified in the Lexington (Ky.) Herald: **Man to fry cook. Must be fast, polite, sober and clean-cut.**

Ad in the Thompsonville (Conn.) Press: **Wanted— Man to wash dishes and two waitresses.**

Ad in the St. Augustine (Fla.) Record: **Holds shirt up and slacks down.**

Furniture-for-sale ad in the Union City (N.J.) Hudson Dispatch: New Bed Blonde $20.

Cherry Valley (N.Y.) News: Want woman to hook rugs and a salesman.

Miami (Fla.) Herald: '46 Chevrolet truck with vegetable peddlers' body. In A-1 condition.

Display ad in the Norristown (Pa.) Times Herald: Bring your bedroom problems to me.

Galena Park (Tex.) Channel Press: Emma—Come on home. All forgiven. My upper plate is still in your purse.

Classified in the Raleigh (N.C.) News & Observer: Steam heated rooms, showers, business girls. Also gentleman.

Ad in the Racine (Wis.) Sunday Bulletin: Like new, 16 gauge shotgun for sale cheap. Also wedding dress with·veil.

Baby-sitting ad in the Palo Atlo (Calif.) Times: Middle-aged woman who enjoys boys by the hour; mostly at night.

Classified ad in the Athens (Ohio) Messenger: Three-room Apartment with bath, man and wife, one furnished, and one unfurnished, all new, reasonable.

Movie ad in the Bloomington (Ind.) Daily Herald: "Every girl should be married" and "Manhandled."

Salt Lake City (Utah) Desert News: House to rent by widow newly painted and renovated with every modern improvement.

Tyndall (S. Dak.) Tribune & Register: Wanted— Second hand typewriter by young lady student with wide carriage.

Room & Board want ad in the Detroit (Mich.) News: Working mother and baby 10 months; day care for baby; good natured tot; non-smoker or drinker.

Under Rooms for Rent in the St. Louis (Mo.) Star Times: Young man—to share double room; or two girls, twin beds.

Classified ad in the Miami (Fla.) Herald: Ann. Heart condition made me make a solemn promise to obey all the commandments of God. I cannot see you again. Zeke.

In Albany (Oreg.) the Greater Oregon ran an unsigned classified ad: If the man who went rushing out the front door of my house the other night without any clothes on will call at my office, he can have his clothes and no questions asked.

In Kansas City, Mo., the Star ran this ad: Wanted: healthy, rugged girl weighing over 300 lbs. to be sawed in half by upcoming prestidigitator; have good act, but present partner is thin and sawing in half routine too short.

In Mexico, N.Y., the Independent carried the personal ad: George, please come home, the children need you, the lawn will need mowing soon and the garden needs a worm like you. Mabel, your loving wife.

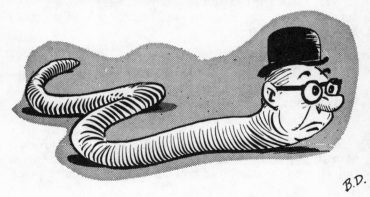

B.D.

Ad in the Salt Lake City (Utah) Desert News: Shoes Too Short? Have Toes Removed To Fit By An Expert.

50

In Liberty, Ky., the Casey County News advertised: To the person who is so destitute as to be forced to take two lengths of garden hose and a sprinkler from the lawn of the First Christian Church—If you will call at the pastor's study, he will give you the five-year guarantee for the hose, your dinner, and any religion that may rub off on you.

Classified in the Cedar Rapids (Iowa) Gazette: For sale, love seat that opens into bed.

In Oakland, Calif., in its classified advertising columns, the Tribune offered: Hollywood bed frame, mattress, springs; wedding veil, reasonable. LO 9-2365.

In the McLeansboro (Ill.) Times-Leader, Mrs. Ebb Hargrave pleaded: Will the person or persons who took all my hens and left the old rooster come and get him. He is lonesome.

In Duluth, Minn., Lucy Ann Susienka inserted a personal ad in the News-Tribune: As far as my husband, Melvin Susienka, not being responsible for my bills, he never was. I have always paid the bills as he usually doesn't work.

In Cheboygan, Mich., a classified advertisement in the Tribune read: For sale: police dog. Will eat anything. Very fond of children.

In St. Peter, Minn., the weekly Herald ran a classified ad: Wanted: Man to handle dynamite. Must be prepared to travel unexpectedly.

In Springfield, Ohio, Victor Wagle, 31, was swamped with calls after he put ads in the Sun and the News: Undependable, sloppy, liar, cheat, drunkard, allergic to work: need job, $75 a week.

In Chattanooga, Tenn., restaurant owner Mitchell Wallace put this ad in the Times: Business for sale. Need money for Orange Bowl game.

In Bloomington, Ill., the Daily Pantagraph carried this classified ad: Highly intelligent fellow . . . lazy, unreliable young man who chews tobacco, has three small children to feed, wants highly paid executive position. . . .

In East Paterson, N.J., the Shopper carried this ad:
For rent—widow would like to share apartment with
another woman, middle-aged. Or gentlemen with references. . . .

*In Ely, Nev., Al Volckart placed a notice in the Ely
Daily Times:* My advertisement of Jan. 24 was an error. I will be responsible for my wife's debts.

The Chagrin Falls (Ohio) Summer Theater advertised "The Respectful Prostitute" with an all professional cast.

Girl as bar maid; bust be attractive. SE 9989—*Advertised in the Seattle (Wash.) Post-Intelligencer.*

*In Atlanta, the Jack Salmon (Realty) Co. advertised
in the Constitution:* Beautiful Estate. . . . Astounding
Value, including two wonderful maids and other interesting features . . . can be seen any time. . . .

Wench for sale—Complete with rope. For further
information call 3081 Rivesville—*Advertised in the
Fairmont West Virginian.*

Family with 1½ small children need 2 bedroom house
—*San Pedro (Calif.) News-Pilot.*

Wedding outfit with cutting torch and tanks. All accessories—*Glendale (Calif.) News-Press.*

*Lost and Found in the Newport News (Va.) Daily
Press:* One man's wallet with T. J. Terney inside.

53

Help Wanted in The New York Times: Saleslady—part or full time work—hosiery and love experience. Apply in person.

Rooms for Rent in the Orlando (Fla.) Sentinel: Teacher qualified in teaching fanatics to share apt.

From the Salt Lake City (Utah) Tribune: Notice to our friends, to bill collectors, radio and TV poll takers, et al: due to our daughter's return from college for the holidays, we expect a 30-minute to three-hour delay on all telephone calls to our residence. Mr. and Mrs. H. H. Fisher.

House for rent in the San Diego (Calif.) Evening Tribune: $65 2 B.R. redecorated children.

Two rooms near school, all home privileges, with widow—*Charleston (W. Va.) Daily Mail.*

Our pies are a threat to any family—*Cape May (N.J.) Star and Wave.*

Rummage sale—Ladies' Auxiliary, having cast off clothes, now invite inspection—*Wildwood-by-the-Sea (N.J.) Independent Record.*

Advertisement in the St. Petersburg (Fla.) Times: Seersucker Wash Pants $2.97 Air-Conditioned.

In Hailey, Idaho, the weekly Times carried this classified advertisement: Personal Notice: If the man who stole my wife at the celebration Monday will agree to pay her expenses, he is welcome to keep her as long as he can. But don't bring her back. E.K.S.

Display ad in the Meriden (Conn.) Record: The Three Little Brothers—Boys' Trousers Will Be Open Saturday From 2 to 4.

An ad in Daily Variety: I surrender. Young man with no agent, no contract, no roles, will give up promising career as actor for interesting job.

From the Columbus (Ohio) Tri-Village News: For sale: 18-foot boat, with two bailing pumps and large tin can. May be seen by appointment. Bring diving mask.

From the Los Angeles Westchester Airport Tribune: Young lady with 1941 Chevrolet desires to meet personable young man mechanically inclined.

A furniture store in Janesville, Wis., advertised: Will the mother whose little boy laid his sucker on an end table come in? She can have the end table for just $1, with sucker still intact.

St. Joseph's Cemetery will be closed for the winter. Residents of this area should take due notice and govern themselves accordingly—*Red Lake Falls (Minn.) Gazette.*

I will not be responsible for debts made only by myself—*Lawrence (Kans.) Daily Journal-World.*

For Sale—Osculating fans—*Champaign-Urbana (Ill.) News-Gazette.*

Wanted—Experienced spotter. Must be sober or married—*Reno (Nev.) Journal.*

Waitress—for full or part time bath and pantry—*Lawrence (Mass.) Eagle-Tribune.*

Man Wanted with Washroom Experiences—*Albuquerque (N. Mex.) Tribune.*

Lovely ranch-type bungalow. Plumbing situated on beautiful landscaped lot—*Vancouver (B.C.) Sun.*

Girl wants sleep in job—*Richmond (Va.) News-Leader.*

Want Child Hitter in my home—*Fort Worth (Tex.) Press.*

Three Rooms, Clean Children O.K.—*Butte (Mont.) Standard.*

Nice 2 bedroom home in shady neighborhood—*Delta Democrat-Times (Greenville, Miss.).*

Ad in the Boston Herald: Hearse. 1937 La Salle. Not a scratch on it. Best thing in the world for a skiing trip.

Need warmth, interest in and experience with girls, and vigorous help—*Wisconsin State Journal (Madison)*.

Dads' Show announcement in a Monrovia (Calif.) daily: If you're a tenor, bass, or barracuda, be at Duarte School at 7:30 p.m. Thursday.

Ad in the Tinker Air Force Base Take-Off: Blonde model available for evening entertainment. ME 2-5154. Bargain TV.

From the De Kalb (Ill.) Daily Chronicle: Day nursery—Expert supervision for ages six weeks to five years. By hour or day. Unreasonable rates for unreasonable children.

Ad in Billboard: Lion tamer wants tamer lion.

From the Hastings & St. Leonards (England) Observer: House to let. Furnished with period pieces from an unfortunate period.

From the Ramey Air Force Base Daily Bulletin: Found: Parakeet. I own cat. HURRY. Call 83256.

Apt. Carpeted living room. Large closets. Natural birth kitchen cabinets—*Springfield (Ill.) Journal-Register.*

Piece goods ad in the San Antonio (Tex.) News headed in big type: LADIES, GET FELT AT SCRIVENER'S.

In San Antonio, this item appeared in the Light: $10 Reward [for] anyone giving name and address of party that removed three-room frame house and barn in rear of 113 North Pecos Street. . .

HEADLINES

In every newspaper office, little men sit around tables and pound out the headlines that your eyes catch first when you pick up your paper. Somewhere between the desk and the machines that set the news in metal type, a slip is sometimes made.

GIRL PASSENGER SAYS SHE WAS NOT BEING KISSED, DRIVER FINED FOR CARELESSNESS—*Salt Lake City (Utah) Tribune.*

SUDDEN FALL IN MEN'S SUITS BRINGS POLICE IN A HURRY—*Wichita Falls (Tex.) Record-News.*

MOTHER OF 12 CHILDREN ADVOCATES RELAXATION—*Michigan City (Mich.) News Dispatch.*

SAYS WOMEN SAME AS MEN IN RED POLAND—*Muncie (Ind.) Star.*

CHURCH FOLKS CONFIDENT OF BEATING HELL—*Somerset (Pa.) American.*

CONGRATULATIONS: 300 HURT—*Albuquerque (N. Mex.) Tribune.*

THEFT OF WENCHES AND OTHER ARTICLES DRAWS SENTENCES—*Dowington (Pa.) Archive.*

NO SQUEEZE EXPECTED IN CORSET INDUS-TRY—*San Diego (Calif.) Evening Tribune.*

BROADCASTERS TO LOOK INTO PLUNGING GOWNS—*Eugene (Oreg.) Register-Guard.*

FATHER OF TEN SHOT; MISTAKEN FOR RAB-BIT—*Ogden (Utah) Standard-Examiner.*

BRIDEGROOM OF THREE MONTHS DIES IN ACTION—*San Antonio (Tex.) Express.*

FRESHMEN WOMEN OUTSTRIP MEN AT I.U.
—*Indianapolis (Ind.) Times.*

SCOUT LEADERS BARBECUE GUESTS—*Syracuse (N.Y.) Herald-Journal.*

HOBO IS APPOINTED FINANCE DIRECTOR—
Huntsville (Ala.) Times.

NIXON FISHES WITH CUT FOOT—*Durham (N.C.) Sun.*

OUTHOUSES AIRED AT COUNCIL MEET—*Onconto County (Wis.) Reporter.*

JOAN CRAWFORD PLANS TO BECOME WOMAN PRODUCER—*Los Angeles Herald Examiner.*

SKELETON IN HOSPITAL WITH VIRUS INFECTION—*Petersburg (Va.) Progress Index.*

WOMAN DIES; MAY LIVE HERE—*Albuquerque (N. Mex.) Journal.*

CEMETERY GROUP PLANS CARD PARTY—*Spokane (Wash.) Inland Register.*

BEDROOMS PROVE QUITE DANGEROUS—*Albuquerque (N. Mex.) Journal.*

MINGLING OF SEXES IN COLLEGE FAVORED 18 TO 7 BY GIRLS AT BOSTON LYING IN HOSPITAL—*Boston (Mass.) Traveler.*

WAXING WIDOWS ALSO WAS GREAT FUN—*Toledo (Ohio) Blade.*

GOOSE GIVEN TO EISENHOWER—*Philadelphia Inquirer.*

ATTORNEY GENERAL URGES CLOSER LOOK AT NUDIST COLONY—*Albuquerque (N. Mex.) Tribune.*

GOP REDISTRICTING THREATENS BREEDING—*Wichita (Kans.) Eagle & Beacon.*

FARMER'S HORSE REPLACED BY CHURCH—*New Bern (N.C.) Journal.*

Two-column front page headline in The New York Times—SPANISH FORBID SCANTY SWIM SUITS. WHEN GRANDFATHER DIES SUDDENLY.

BREAKS WHISKEY BOTTLE OVER FATHER'S HEAD, JAILED FOR RECKLESS DRIVING—*Vincennes (Ind.) Sun Commercial.*

5 NUDES PINCHED AT STAG SHOW—*Los Angeles (Calif.) Mirror.*

AUTOS KILLING 110 A DAY; LET'S RESOLVE TO DO BETTER—*Boston (Mass.) Globe.*

TAKES BRIDE AFTER FATAL N.J. ACCIDENT—*Brockton (Mass.) Enterprise & Times.*

ROY S. BLANK DIES SOON AFTER FUNERAL—*Omaha (Nebr.) World-Herald.*

NURSE MAY BE BEST FOR SLEEPING PROBLEM—*Hartford (Conn.) Times.*

"NUMBER PLEASE" GIRL QUITS AFTER 42 YEAR STINK—*Miami (Fla.) Herald.*

KIMONO REVEALS WOMAN'S SECRETS—*Hyannis (Mass.) Cape Cod Standard Times.*

BRIDE IN MT. CARMEL CEMETERY—*Middletown (N.Y.) Times-Herald.*

FATHER SEEKS TO HAVE CHILDREN PERI- ODICALLY—*Hazleton (Pa.) Plain Speaker.*

MAYOR WILL DEVOTE TWO DAYS TO WOMEN —*St. Louis (Mo.) Globe-Democrat.*

FORMER GIRL WINS TOP HONORS IN DOG SHOW—*Waverly (Ohio) Watchman.*

UW MALES HAVE FEWER CHILDREN, WOM- EN MORE—*Cheyenne (Wyo.) Eagle.*

NUDISTS TAKE OFF FOR CONVENTION— *Grand Forks (N. Dak.) Herald.*

SOUTH CAROLINA GIRL IS NEW MISS USA— BLONDE LOST CLOTHES ON WAY TO CONTEST —*Toledo (Ohio) Times.*

FATHER MAY HAVE CHILDREN IS VIEW— *Cincinnati (Ohio) Times Star.*

WOMAN AND CHILD HURT IN BUSINESS SEC- TION—*Kane (Pa.) Republican.*

MAMIE LEAVES COLD BED—*Baylor (Tex.) Lariat.*

TWO HEADED BABY RECALLS SIMILAR BIRTH IN 1870—*Milwaukee (Wis.) Sentinel.*

NIGHTWEAR LOOKS LIKE PLAY CLOTHES—
Appleton (Wis.) Post-Crescent.

**GIRL BECOMES METHODIST AFTER DELI-
CATE OPERATION—***Bergen (N.J.) Evening Record.*

LOST WIFE FOUND IN SUIT—*New York World-Telegram and Sun.*

GRANDMA TOLD TO PRODUCE INDIAN TOTS
—*Ft. Lauderdale (Fla.) Daily News.*

GRANDSON BORN TO JACK BENNY—*Philadelphia (Pa.) Inquirer.*

IKE EXPECTING—*Durham (N.C.) Sun.*

MOTHER OF 12 PUTS OFF MARRIAGE—*San Jose (Calif.) Mercury.*

GIRLS WITH TORSOS TOLD TO DROP BLUE JEANS IN PUBLIC—*Clarksburg (W.Va.) Telegram.*

DOGS DENIED BITE OF CITY WORKERS—*El Paso (Tex.) Herald-Post.*

MALE UNDERWEAR WILL REVEAL NEW, COLORFUL SIGHTS—*Norfolk (Nebr.) Daily News.*

EXPERIMENTS NOT WHOLLY UNPLEASANT TO ENGAGED COUPLE—*Lancaster (Pa.) Intelligencer Journal.*

COUPLE GOES TO PARTY, COMES HOME WITH BABY—*Flint (Mich.) Journal.*

DEATH OF NEWLYWEDS ORPHANS 8 CHIL-DREN—*Norfolk (Va.) Ledger-Dispatch.*

WOMAN JAILED FOR 11 MONTHS PREGNANT—*Milton (Pa.) Evening Standard.*

MAYOR ORDERS MACHINES TO REPLACE MOTHERS—*Hartford (Conn.) Courant.*

NEVADA HAS WATER BUT IT CAN'T BE USED UNTIL FOUND—*Austin (Nev.) Reese River Reveille.*

TRAVEL TIP TO HONEYMOONERS: GO TO VIRGIN ISLANDS—*Philadelphia (Pa.) Inquirer.*

MORTUARY SUES MAN WHO CAME BACK AFTER FUNERAL—*Datil (N. Mex.) Roundup.*

VERMONTER SAYS MORE SKIING GOES ON IN WINTER—*Springfield (Mass.) Union.*

EXPECTANT MOTHER 23, IS ANXIOUS FOR FACTS—*Columbia (S.C.) State.*

WIFE CHARGES HUSBAND KILLED HER FOR MONEY—*Niles (Ohio) Times.*

BRIDEGROOM NERVOUS SO POLICE HELP—*Los Angeles Times.*

LA MESA CORSET IN NEW LOCATION—*La Mesa (Calif.) News.*

PRIEST TURNS HOLY ROLLER AS HIS CAR TURNS TURTLE—*Iron (Mich.) Reporter.*

WOMEN SPEND MORE TIME IN KITCHEN DESPITE ADVANCES—*Harrisburg (Pa.) Sun Patriot News.*

18 CHILDREN THERE AS PARENTS MARRY —*Ridgewood (N.J.) Sunday News.*

JURY HUNG IN BRA CASE—*Charleston (W.Va.) Gazette.*

ANGRY CASTRO LEAVES HOTEL, GOES TO HAREM—*Idaho Falls (Idaho) Post-Register.*

BARREN WIFE LEARNS TO BEAR CHILDREN FOR AMAZING HUSBAND—*Huntington (W.Va.) Advertiser.*

The Pittsburgh (Pa.) Press headlined: DIAPER THIEF LEAVES 150 BABIES WITH NO PLACE TO GO.

Flanked by two comic panels, this headline took the laughs in the New Brunswick (N.J.) Sunday Home News: MOTORMAN WELL AUTOPSY REVEALS.

From the Philadelphia (Pa.) Bulletin: GIRLS SEEK BIRTHS ON U.S. TRACK TEAM.

DISCHARGE FOR DADS OVER 3—*Pittsburgh (Pa.) Sun-Telegraph.*

SECRET OF CHARM: LEAVE TROUSERS HOME WHEN YOU TRAVEL—*Charleston (W. Va.) Daily Mail.*

HORSES TO RUN EVEN IF THEY HAVE TO WALK—*Boston (Mass.) Herald.*

From coast to coast traveled the Wakefield (Mass.) Daily Item's headline: WOMEN ARE URGED TO FLATTEN CANS, *but then came a lulu from the Malden (Mass.) Evening News:* MAYOR MCCARTHY SITS ON THRONE ALL MORNING.

ARSON SCHOOL GRADUATES 51 STUDENTS—
Winston-Salem (N.C.) Journal.

Neatest trick! A St. Louis woman, born 20 years past on February 29, gave birth to a daughter on February 29, 1944. The Globe-Democrat carried the following headline in the early edition: WOMAN BORN FEBRUARY 29 HAS BABY SAME DAY.

Columnist Walter Winchell was surprised to read this headline in 1944 in the Somerset (Pa.) American: WINCHELL DEFIES HOFFMAN AND DIES.

DROWNED MAN JUST RESTING OFFICERS FIND—*Titusville (Pa.) Herald.*

RECIPE FOR SUCCESS: HOW TO COOK A HUSBAND—*Seattle (Wash.) Times.*

MAN WHOSE HEART STOPPED BEATING TO TAKE IT EASY—*Macon (Ga.) News.*

An Associated Press wire story, carried in big headlines on page one out West, said: ALL DRAFTED MEN WILL BE FATHERS SOON.

BAPTISTS SET DOPE SPEAKER—*Glendale (Calif.) News-Press.*

MISSING WOMAN GOES TO AMARILLO—*El Paso (Tex.) Times.*

In 1940 John Chapman's "Mainly About Manhattan" column in the New York Daily News printed the following item: The Montreal Herald scurried around like crazy calling back first editions of the paper the day after Britain's new boat arrived, because of a typo in the head: ELECTRIC GIRDLE ON QUEEN ELIZABETH IS NAVEL SECRET.

SCOUT TROOP SLATES FATHER-SIN BANQUET—*Gastonia (N.C.) Gazette.*

MISS BOOZER WINS TEMPERANCE PRIZE—*Charlotte (N.C.) Observer.*

CEMETERY SITE IS APPROVED BY BODY—
Manhattan (Kans.) Mercury.

GRAHAM COUPLE IS ENTERTAINED ON 50TH
WEDDING—*Durham (N.C.) Morning Herald.*

CHILDREN TO GET SHOT ON TUESDAY—
Hackensack (N.J.) Bergen Evening Record.

JUNE IS THE MONTH FOR COWS—AS WELL
AS PRETTY BRIDES—*Portales (N. Mex.) Tribune.*

ADULTERY WITH WIFE CAUSED PASTOR'S
DEATH—*Edinburg (Tex.) Daily Review.*

UNITED GAS CO. COOKING GIRLS—*Welsh
(La.) Citizen.*

MASSAGES FROM FRIENDS HELP WATTS
AND WIFE—*Clarksburg (W. Va.) Exponent Telegram.*

BOYS AND GIRLS SAME ALL OVER—*Boston
Globe.*

HOW TO COOK HUSBANDS AND OTHER RECIPES—*Mexia (Tex.) Senior Citizen.*

THEY USED HEADS IN EARLY FOOTBALL—
Los Angeles Times.

MEN ALUMNI HAVE MORE CHILDREN THAN
WOMEN, REPORT SAYS—*Los Angeles Times.*

CASE OF STOLEN WHISKEY EXPECTED TO GO TO JURY—*New Brunswick (N.J.) Sunday Home News.*

INFANT'S ARRIVAL IMPELS PARENTS TO SEEK NEW RECREATION IDEAS—*Appleton (Wis.) Post-Crescent.*

BE A WIFE FIRST THEN A MOTHER—*New Orleans (La.) Times-Picayune.*

JANITOR CHARGED WITH BATTERY—*Cincinnati (Ohio) Times Star.*

MAY BREAKFAST COMING UP—*Council Bluffs (Iowa) Nonpareil.*

SCRANTON BUS TALKS MONDAY—*Hazleton (Pa.) Plain Speaker.*

MAN WITH LEG BURNS BETTER—*Spokane (Wash.) Spokesman-Review.*

FIND GIRLS ARE NOT EQUIPPED TO BE MOTHERS—*Chicago Tribune.*

PASTOR RAPS FAILURE TO USE WOMEN—
Buffalo (N.Y.) Courier-Express.

CHILD LIBRARIAN PLANS TO RETIRE—*Syracuse (N.Y.) Herald-Journal.*

IT'S BUYER'S MARKET; GET YOUR CASKET NOW—*Los Angeles Daily News.*

TELL HOW DEANNA DURBIN GOT START IN BETTER BABIES—*Los Angeles Herald & Express.*

PAINT, WALLPAPER MEET THURSDAY—*Los Angeles Daily News.*

HALF PLUMBERS BACK ON JOB—*Sacramento (Calif.) Union.*

WOMEN CONSIDER THINKING—*Richwood (W. Va.) News Leader.*

UPSET STOMACH LICKED BY IKE; BUSY WEEK—*Durham (N.C.) Sun.*

SALESMAN'S WIFE TO BE DISCUSSED—*Houston (Tex.) Press.*

FUNERAL DIRECTORS AT REFRESHER COURSE—*Fort Dodge (Iowa) Messenger & Chronicle.*

STEEL FIGURE WILL ADDRESS CONCRETE MEN—*Dallas (Tex.) Morning News.*

ACTRESS SLAPS GIRL WITH ITALIAN MATE
—*Durham (N.C.) Sun.*

JOS. BLANK DIES; TO LEAVE ON VISIT TO
GERMANY TODAY—*Belleville (Ill.) Daily Advocate.*

SINATRA EXHAUSTED; MAY SEE AVA LATER
—*Los Angeles Daily News.*

CAFE OPERATOR HELD IN BEER CASE—*Nashville Tennessean.*

MULE KICKS YOUTH, ANOTHER SHOOTS
SELF—*Birmingham (Ala.) News.*

QUEEN ELIZABETH OK DESPITE DENT IN
SIDE—*Cortland (N.Y.) Standard.*

FOR 40 YEARS HE PLAYED WITH HIS WIFE
ON VAUDEVILLE CIRCUITS—*Franklin (Mass.)
Sentinel.*

MOSQUITO BITES PART OF HIS JOB—*Racine
(Wis.) Sunday Bulletin.*

ESTHER SHEDS SWIM SUIT FOR MORE DRA-
MATIC ROLES—*El Paso (Tex.) Herald-Post.*

SINGLE MEN SHOW APTITUDE FOR PARENT-
HOOD—*Kalamazoo (Mich.) Gazette.*

MAN GETS HONEY UNDER BEDROOM FLOOR
—*Stockton (Calif.) Record.*

Thanks to an alert proofreader, the Sacramento (Calif.) Union didn't use this head that wouldn't fit:
PORTLAND RABBI GIVES BIRTH TO 30 BUNNIES.

ODD GIRLS HOLD PARTY—*Rome (N.Y.) Sentinel.*

SOCIETY

Out of the women's and society pages of your local newspaper.

Lettuce won't turn brown if you put your head in a plastic bag before placing it in the refrigerator—*Wildwood-by-the-Sea (N.J.) Cape May County News.*

Dean Blank read the wedding service, and it was nice to see Mrs. Blank and daughter, Catherine, bath at the ceremony—*Erie (Pa.) Dispatch.*

MISS SCHELL ADVISES BREATHING FOR BEAUTY—*Washington (D.C.) Star.*

HOTHOUSE PANTS, USED AS TABLE DECORATIONS, WERE AWARDED AS DOOR PRIZES—*Conneaut (Ohio) News-Herald.*

Your problems: Child has no place at mother's first wedding—*El Paso (Tex.) Times.*

Shorts return to Fargo after attending wedding—
Langdon (N. Dak.) Cavalier County Republican.

Twice a bridegroom and finally a bride–at least for
last night–was Miss Blank—*West Chester (Pa.)
Daily Local News.*

She was the only girl the Duke danced with. "He
told me I had the most wonderful," she said later with
a sigh—*Cape May (N.J.) Star and Wave.*

Hostess never bothers to dress for card party—
Springfield (Ohio) Daily News.

But we try to avoid the fraction that might come
from being together too much—*The Newton (Kans.)
Kansan.*

At the annual all women's church party, Mrs. Blank
will give the medication—*Winfield (Kans.) Daily
Courier.*

Refreshments of punch, bookies, sandwiches and
salted nuts were served—*New Bern (N.C.) Sun-Jour-
nal.*

Additional greenery was used on the main table, and
smaller tables were decorated with rustic bottles and
candles entwined with Mrs. Blank, Mrs. Smith, Mrs.
Black, Mrs. Blue—*Charlotte (N.C.) Observer.*

Following the ceremony, a wedding supper was hell
at the home—*Pittsburg (Kans.) Headlight.*

Their bouquets were of deep pink people, tied with white ribbon—*Rib Lake (Wis.) Herald.*

School lunch menus include fried children and gravy —*Sterling (Colo.) Advocate.*

A garden setting was based on motifs of old and familiar melodies surrounded by a low white picket fence—*Newton (Kans.) Kansan.*

Announcement in the Louisville (Ky.) Courier-Journal: The ladies of the Cherry Street Church have discarded clothing of all kinds.

Giddings (Tex.) News: The bridegroom's mother, Harold Garrett of Dallas, served as best man.

Hartford (Conn.) Courant: Miss Dush is the financée of Mr. George W. Johnson also of Mr. Salvatore Carpenteri of Henry Street.

Child care described in the Dorothy Dix column in the Indianapolis (Ind.) Star: They fed and clothed them, killed them when they were good and spanked them when they were bad.

Beauty note in the McAllen (Tex.) Evening Monitor: With or without a bathing suit Barbara Blank is a mighty pretty girl.

Unpleasant smoke that sometimes arises when cooking hot cakes can be avoided by tying some salt in a bag and rubbing the girdle with this instead of greasing it—*Charlotte (N.C.) News.*

From Josephine Lowman's "Why Grow Old" column as it appeared in the Chattanooga (Tenn.) Times: Remember, too, that it is always better to be undressed than overdressed.

From the Emily Post column in the Washington (D.C.) Star: At that time the invitations were ready to mail and her lovely hot water wedding dress ready; her attendants also had their organza dresses bought.

Caught by a society reporter of the Waterbury (Conn.) American in checking a wedding story: The gown is of slipper satin redingote style with a standing collar, open from the waist down.

Society note in the Batavia (N.Y.) Daily News: A bathroom shower was given the bride.

Glorious country at that season for the leaves will be turning and yes sweaters will be worn over almost everything—*Jacksonville (Fla.) Journal.*

Wedding story in the Scarsdale (N.Y.) Inquirer: The groom's father was dressed in mauve lace and a shell pink hat.

Members are urged to bring eligible women who might wish to become mothers—*Fredericksburg (Va.) Free Lance-Star.*

Caption over a girl's picture in the society section of
the New York Herald Tribune: Engaged in Flushing.

A recent bride, in filling out her wedding data blank for the Waterbury (Conn.) American, wrote under "Decorations for reception": Four roses and three feathers.

They played cards after the meeting. Mrs. Blank got high and Mrs. Doe got low—*Mountain Home* (Idaho) *News*.

*Engagement announcements in the Brooklyn (N.Y.)
Eagle's society page once included this item:* Mr. and
Mrs. ____ announce the betrayal of their daughter,
Miss ____ to Ensign ____.

Society editor leaves town: If Mrs. Keith smelled as
sweet as she always looks, 'twould be over-powering
for fair.

*The Ada (Okla.) Evening News finally ran the kind
of society item it had been itching to carry for years
when its society editor, Juanita Cooper, was married
to Private Watson Benge. Under a two-column picture
of the bride was this caption:* Three days in a beauty
shop and about ten thousand dollars worth of high-
powered photographic equipment were all that were
required to produce this flattering view of Miss Juanita
Cooper.

The story said: The wedding is scheduled to be a
simple, "get it over quick" affair. Plans call for the
home to be modestly decorated with arrangements of
cut flowers, a general atmosphere of tense nervousness,
and the weeping of delighted relatives. Only a few
intimates, not counting stowaways and neighborhood
urchins, will sit through the death watch.

The bride (Cooper) will wear—unless she thinks of
something cuter—a blue afternoon frock, fashioned
with fitted basque, a white lace collar and pockets. No-
body knows what the pockets are for. She will wear a
flaring skirt. Since she is an army bride she will wear
navy accessories, to be fair to both services. Her cor-
sage will be of white and pink carnations and sweet
peas, along with a notebook and pencil to enable her
to cover her own wedding properly for the paper. Her
"something old," in addition to a pair of silk stockings,
will be a lavaliere cameo which her mother will certainly be lucky to get back.

To top the whole afternoon's entertainment, the
bride's parents will give a reception immediately after
the ceremony, provided either Juanita or Watson is
conscious.

*The Ogden (Utah) Standard-Examiner society edi-
tor's heart almost missed a beat when she read:* The
young lady who was going to be married, spent three
months getting her torso ready.

B.D.

*In a story about a society woman's mystery death
the A.P. trunk wire carried, and at least one newspaper printed, in 1938:*
Mrs. Davidson, who attended Radcliffe College 20
years ago, never regained consciousness.

Under the etiquette column called "*Mind Your Manners*" in the *Pittsfield (Mass.) Eagle* appeared a group of typical questions and answers headed by the statement: Test your knowledge of correct social usage.

Question Number Three was: Is it good manners to pick up a friend's baby and kill him?

The answer was: No.

Undignified behavior of male present at wedding of daughter as reported in the Villager, Greenwich Village, New York, on October 12, 1938:

The bride was given in marriage by her father, wearing her mother's wedding gown.

SPORTS

Found on the sports pages . . .

Associated Press account of the Purdue vs. Michigan football game: Purdue wasted little time in scoring after recovering a fumbled punt. . . . four days later Schmaling broke over from the 1-yard line.

FOOTBALL TEAMS BARBECUE GUESTS—*Corpus Christi (Tex.) Caller.*

Sports quote in the Raleigh (N.C.) News & Observer: You don't lose the coordination of four eyes, wrists and legs when you go back to hitting.

Outcome of a boxing match, as reported by the Roanoke (Va.) World-News: One official voted a draw and the other two spit on the winner.

Halfback Tony Waters electrified the crowd with a 994-yard punt return. He collapsed in the end zone after he scored—*Austin (Tex.) Statesman.*

90

Texas, the nation's No. 1 team, was trailing the cadets 663 to 3, late in the third quarter of their first football meeting, when Key broke loose—*Denver (Colo.) Rocky Mountain News.*

Headline on a sports story in the Pittsburgh (Pa.) Press regarding a new player, named Ted Beard:
BEARD WILL GROW ON PIRATE FANS.

Happy Buc fans ate 41,000 hot dogs at a recent doubleheader drawing 32,346 fans. Also, 27,000 bags of peanuts, 26,000 ice cream bars, 30,000 soft drinks, 18,000 score cards and 7,500 cushions—*Chattanooga (Tenn.) Times.*

Billy Blank, Utah 6-9 sophomore sensation, didn't see action until this part of the game, and he didn't start the second half. But he was impressive in his time out—*Albuquerque (N. Mex.) Journal.*

The football players were the happiest. They achieved the best girl record in the school's history, six wins, a tie and two losses—*Ambler (Pa.) Gazette.*

Each team committed sex errors in the wild game, and only seven of the 14 runs scored were earned—*Bridgeport (Conn.) Post.*

Roy Sievers hit his fifth home for the Senators with nine aboard in the fourth inning—*Providence (R.I.) Journal.*

The Japanese team wants $2,500 plus broad and room—*Gastonia (N.C.) Gazette.*

In a sports story of a basketball game, the Bergen Evening Record, Hackensack (N.J.), reported: The Cliffside lad also played a good portion of the second half and impressed the huge crowd with his work under blankets.

Essegian hit the headlines during the 1959 World Series with two inch home runs—*Philadelphia Evening Bulletin*.

Sports writer for New England. Will be required to do some general sporting—*Editor & Publisher*.

Four plays later he ran around his right end for three years in the end zone on a bootleg play—*Mount Vernon (Ohio) News.*

As part of a straight report on a girls' baseball game, the Ogden (Utah) Times sports page said: Everything was going fine until the last half of the fifth when all the bags got loaded.

Sports report in the Columbus (Ga.) Ledger: The Butler boys revenged their girls' loss by drowning the Unadilla boys 40-34.

Then the Bulldogs staged a long march, of 73 years, to go on to score again—*The New York Times.*

With rebounding spit after two flops this season, Minnesota's football squad went on the offense—*Iowa City (Iowa) Daily Iowan.*

Wisser carried the ball 17 times for a total of 72 years—*East Palestine (Ohio) Daily Leader.*

The Associated Press gave Stan Musial quite a record in 1947 when he was adjudged winner of the National League batting honors. Among his achievements, according to the A.P. wire, were: the most singles, 142; the most doubles, 50; and the most triplets, 20.

When a sports writer for the Detroit (Mich.) News came up with two byline stories on the same page, the composing room took special note of it. One story was By Sam Green. *The other was* By Same Green.

The National League voted both baseball clubs permission to move to California if they wash—*Portland (Ore.) Oregonian.*

BEHIND THE SCENE

Anecdotes of and from newspapers throughout the country. . . .

She called the Tulsa (Okla.) World and asked for the make-up editor, having heard that newspapers had such persons on their staff. John Booker, make-up editor, answered the telephone.

"Could you tell me please what store sells —— rouge?" inquired the sweet young thing.

Embarrassed though they must have been, the San Francisco staff of the Associated Press forgot their personal feelings to put this one on the wires on September 21, 1939: "San Francisco, Sept. 21—(AP)—Perspiring editors in the Associated Press office loosened their collars and wondered if they were in California or the Midwest as they turned out heat stories and referred doubtingly to a weather report stating that the temperature was only 97.

"A copy boy saved the situation by turning off a radiator which had been going full blast."

The late Charles Driscoll, McNaught Syndicate columnist, wrote a lead while flying from the West: "In flight, Arizona to New York, Sept. 29—Thinking out loud: Wonder why I always enjoy having a baby on the ship."

96

Disappointed reader writes a letter to the editor: "Editor the Pittsburgh Press: I have been reading Dale Carnegie's column for almost a year now, but I'm still on relief. Frank Schafer."

We seem to have heard this before, but we have a clipping to prove it appeared in the Uniontown (Pa.) Evening Genius on a Thanksgiving Eve. Under a boxed, front-page Thanksgiving poem titled "All Should Be Thankful" ran this line: "Count your many blessings and BE THANKFUL. No issues of the Genius Thursday."

The death of Paul Y. Anderson recalls that, long after his fame was established in St. Louis, he was sent by a petulant city desk to cover a dog show.

He resented the assignment and turned in only a paragraph which went about like this: "Well, we are having a dog show at the Auditorium. It opened today. There are a lot of dogs there and a lot of people went to see them. The dogs didn't bite the people and the people didn't bite the dogs."

The city desk threw the story on the floor but Managing Editor Bovard rescued it and the paragraph appeared on the editorial page.

Anderson received $2, the amount then being paid reporters by the paper for published editorials.

The cub reporter of the Albia (Iowa) Republican who was assigned to cover the class play of the high school came in for his share of literary fame when the following turned up in his story: "The auditorium was filled with expectant mothers eagerly awaiting the appearance of their offspring."

"We get some mighty funny stuff sometimes from our rural correspondents," writes a state editor, "but the funniest paragraph which has come into our office in a long time was from a village a few miles away. The item read like this: 'Mrs. Black has presented the Boy Scout troop with a stuffed barn owl in memory of her late husband.'"

A newspaperman's wife was unhappy because she had only one house key, so she took his key ring to have duplicates made. When she got home from the locksmith's she still had only one house key but in addition three keys to the Chicago Herald and Examiner's men's wash room.

It was a few days before the general election of 1936 when the Rev. Golder Lawrence, pastor, First Methodist Church, Phoenix, Arizona, telephoned the Phoenix Republic office and said, in substance:

"I want to thank your paper for the error made in the story announcing my Sunday services."

A startled reporter gulped once or twice and asked why the minister was pleased if the story had been in error.

"It's like this," said Pastor Lawrence. "My sermon topic was 'What Jesus saw in a Publican.' But in the newspaper it appeared as 'What Jesus saw in a Republican.' I had the biggest audience for my sermon that I've addressed in many weeks!"

The reporter who covered the coroner's office for the Pittsburgh (Pa.) Post-Gazette dropped in on his beat one day to find everybody in the morgue busy. And so when the phone rang he answered it.

The excited voice of a woman asked: "Do you people have a missing man in the morgue who is five feet six inches tall, weighs 159 pounds, wearing a blue serge suit and stutters?"

Without thinking, the reporter repeated the question to one of the deputy coroners.

"No," answered the deputy, "we couldn't have him. None of the men laid out in the back stutters."

One paper insists on looking up all wedding intentions for stories on prospective marriages.

A reporter called up the bride-to-be's home and asked for Mary.

"Mary's married," the voice on the other end answered.

"Well, can you tell me how I can get in touch with her?" queried the newshawk.

"It won't do you any good," barked the other voice. "She's happy with her husband."

One of the Salt Lake City (Utah) Desert News reporters, covering an Alcoholics Anonymous meeting, called in to the rewrite man. He started out with a "quote," and then, in his concentration, forgot to tell the girl who was taking dictation where to end the quote. She interrupted him to ask: "Do you want to end the quote here?"

"Oh, yes," he exclaimed, "I guess I've had one quote too many."

The Gainesville (Fla.) Sun tells this one on its "customers": An inebriate staggered out of a night club into a car of the Florida Highway Patrol. Finally discovering whose car he was in, he began to offer excuses to the patrolmen. When asked about his occupation, the stranger tipsily offered: "I work for the Gainesville Sun."

"What's your position on the paper?" he was queried.

"I'm a subscriber," was the reply.

Bill Moyes, radio columnist in the Portland (Ore.) Oregonian, told of a prominent businessman who had attended a stag party where there was a strip-tease act. When he told his wife about it, she asked: "But didn't she wear a thing?"

"Only shoes," the man replied. Their three-year-old daughter, who had been listening, inquired: "What color shoes, Daddy?"

A well-known managing editor, who was very proud of his brilliant staff, was chagrined to learn that after hours they often drank to excess in a nearby tavern.

He got them together one afternoon, and gave them a talk on the evil of their ways. Then, taking a worm from an envelope, he dropped it into a glass of water. The worm swam around vigorously.

He then thrust the worm into another glass containing gin. The worm soon expired.

"Now," he said, "Can you fellows tell me the moral of this illustration?"

"Yes sir," said Pete.

"Well, tell those dumbbells what it is, and stand up so they can see you."

"As I see it," said Pete, "The moral of this illustration is that if I drink plenty of gin, I won't have worms."

Cometh another variation of "there wasn't any wedding." A high-school football game was held between teams from Odem and Mathis, Texas. The sports editor of the Corpus Christi Caller Times waited patiently for the Odem correspondent to send in the score. The deadline passed, and no story. The next day the Odem correspondent dropped into the office of the Caller Times. Asked why she hadn't sent the score in, she blandly replied: "It was just a tie; I didn't think it counted. The score was 6 to 6."

Intimidation of the press in a slightly new form was disclosed in a letter received by the editor of the Everyday Magazine of the St. Louis Post-Dispatch.

The letter: "In your food report today you stated that cauliflower was a good buy but my mother went to eight stores today looking for it and it has definitely been high-priced. If you continue to print such things in your newspaper, I will stop borrowing it. Yours truly, Jeanette Cook."

They still talk about this one in Minneapolis. When a present-day reporter from the Minneapolis Star Journal was breaking in, a mental patient jumped from the fifth floor of General Hospital, across the street from the newspaper building. The city editor sent him to cover.

The cub returned a few minutes later, visibly impressed by his first contact as a newspaperman with tragedy and violent death.

"Yup," he blurted, "he's dead, all right. He was already turning black when I got there."

"He should be black," retorted the city editor: "He's a Negro."

During World War II, the English War Office admitted, according to the United Press under a London dateline, that a publicity release referring to the various colors of pass tickets issued to the military forces doesn't mean literally what it says in this instance: "Members of the Women's Auxiliary Territorial Service will show their pink forms whenever called upon to do so."

A proud father called up the Salt Lake City Tribune editorial department to report the birth of triplets. The reporter didn't quite catch the message and asked, "Will you repeat that?"

Proud parent replied: "Not if I can help it!"

A certain reporter on a Southern daily noted for his carousing called his city editor one day to report off sick.

"Say, I'm sick today and can't come to work," he said. "Do you believe me or do I have to come down there and show you I'm drunk."

A Chicago Tribune contributor had an idea: "I notice that the government has decided to restrict weather forecasts in order to keep information from the enemy. Why not continue to publish them and fool the enemy like they do us?"

One of the older Silurians, commenting on a talk by the late columnist George Sokolsky, then of the New York Sun, recalled an editorial he had written in his early days of journalism.

"That's a fine editorial," commented his editor. "It's great. First you call him a b_____, then you gradually become abusive."

Few correspondents, inadvertently or otherwise, are as honest in tips to the editor as Mrs. Lena Leece, who told the Petoskey (Mich.) Evening News: "I will not send in any news for Saturday because I expect to be so sick I cannot write and will go fishing instead."

James S. Lindsley, A.P. writer, once datelined a story: "Aboard a bar stool at Ciro's Restaurant, Hollywood . . ."

Employees of the circulation department of an Anderson, Indiana, paper thought they'd seen most everything until a subscriber ordered discontinuance of the paper.

Complained the subscriber: "There isn't enough paper in it to wrap lunches for my kids in school."

Tonic or sedative? While his mother summers on Cape Cod, a ten-year-old boy is at camp in Maine. To the mother there came this message in bold lettering on a post card: "Dear Mom: I have Diarrhea now. Would you please send me the Falmouth Enterprise after you have Red it. Love, Charles."

"Memphis, Tenn., August 26, 1942: City Editor Neil Adams, of the Memphis Press-Scimitar, decided to spend his vacation at home—you know, loafing, odd jobs, man-about-the-house stuff.

"The first day he decided to fix the attic fan. He fell through the ceiling. Next day he tackled the hedge— ran into a hornets' nest. Disgusted, he went horseback riding—and fell off."

One of the younger reporters on the Baltimore Evening Sun was writing a short bit about a Negro woman who had been beaten up by her husband. He turned it over to the overnight editor and walked back to his desk.

Suddenly the editor laughed uproariously.

The reporter had written this lead: "A colored woman stood before Magistrate Harry W. Allers in police court with a black eye."

Some years ago Dave Gibson was day city editor and Perc' Trussell night city editor of the Baltimore Sun. A sweet young thing, who knew none of the terms or practices of a city room, was given a tryout and handed an assignment by an assistant city editor.

"Go to this address," he said, handing her a memorandum, "and see the woman whose name is given. Tell her we want to quote her on this subject." Then his voice became stern.

"Don't be late! Hurry back—and write it for the bulldog."

The girl took the memo, but hesitated. Finally, with obvious embarrassment, she replied: "I'll go immediately, and I'll hurry right back. But tell me, please. who is the bulldog—Mr. Trussell or Mr. Gibson?"

108

A middle-aged couple were so anxious to keep their marriage out of the papers that they didn't bring witnesses when appearing before the probate judge at Moscow, Idaho.

Two strangers in the office were called on to assist. When they left, the groom asked who his aides were. "Just a couple of reporters on the Daily Idahonian," the judge replied. Needless to say, the marriage was well publicized.

THE BOOK
AND ITS PERPETRATORS

DICK HYMAN *is a native New Yorker. He was Publicity Director for Robert L. Ripley and his "Believe It or Not," and his columns appeared regularly in magazines like* American *and* Colliers. *He later established his own publicity business. He is the author of* COCKEYED AMERICANA, THE TRENTON PICKLE ORDINANCE, *and* POTOMAC WIND AND WISDOM *for this press. People continue to do strange and funny things, and Dick Hyman continues to help us laugh at ourselves.*

BOB DUNN *is a native of Newark, New Jersey. He was an artist on the* Newark Ledger, *and then moved to King Features Syndicate in the comic-art department where he eventually succeeded Jimmy Hatlo as the cartoonist of the popular feature, "They'll Do It Everytime." He has had two television shows, and has authored several books. He was unanimously elected president of the National Cartoonists' Society in 1965.*